Cheeky Monkey's
Big Race

by Anne Cassidy

Illustrated by Lisa Smith

W

FRANKLIN WATTS

LONDON•SYDNEY

Franklin Watts
338 Euston Road
London
NW1 3BH

Franklin Watts Australia
Level 17/207 Kent Street
Sydney
NSW 2000

A CIP catalogue record for this book is available
from the British Library.

ISBN 978 1 4451 1612 9 (hbk)
ISBN 978 1 4451 1618 1 (pbk)

Series Editor: Jackie Hamley
Series Advisor: Catherine Glavina
Series Designer: Peter Scoulding

Printed in China

Franklin Watts is a divison of
Hachette Children's Books,
an Hachette UK company.
www.hachette.co.uk

Wendy was getting her car ready for the race.

GRAND RACE ON WHEELS

1st prize

Monkey wanted to take part.
"I'm going to win the cake,"
he said.

"Don't be silly," Wendy said, crossly. "I will win it."

The race began.

Wendy drove off.

The monkey was fast.

He went past Wendy.

Then his wheels fell off.

"Ha, ha!" Wendy shouted.

"I'll win that cake."

She passed him.

Monkey found a scooter.

He rode quickly.

Wendy was far away.
He wanted to catch up
with her car.

Wendy had to stop for petrol. Monkey laughed.

He rushed past.

And knocked into a tree!

Wendy was going up a hill.
The monkey was on a
skateboard.

A bus passed. The monkey jumped onto it.

15

Monkey was at the top of the hill! "I'm going to win!"

Wendy caught up to him. The monkey went down the hill very fast.

Too fast!

He splashed into the lake!

Wendy was close to the end of the race.

She went as fast as
she could.

But the monkey was
wearing roller skates.

He caught up with her!

They were both winners!

"Where's the cake?"

Monkey cried.

"I want that cake!"
Wendy shouted.

27

Wendy and Monkey raced for the cake!

Puzzle 1

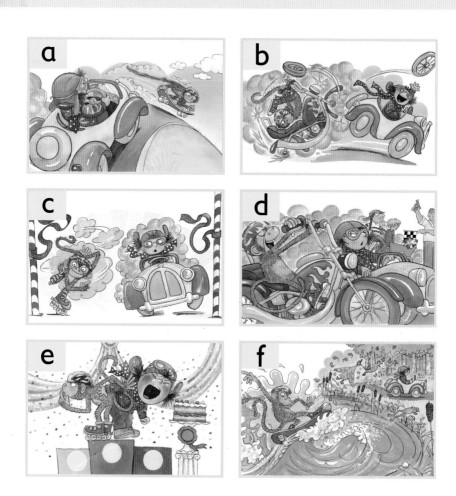

Put these pictures in the correct order.
Now tell the story in your own words.
How short can you make the story?

Puzzle 2

excited   shocked

happy

sad   thrilled

upset

Choose the word which best describes each character. Can you think of any more? Pretend to be one of the characters!

Answers

Puzzle 1

The correct order is:

1d, 2b, 3a, 4f, 5c, 6e

Puzzle 2

Wendy   The correct word is shocked.

The incorrect words are excited, happy.

Monkey   The correct word is thrilled.

The incorrect words are sad, upset.